1.2.3 counting under the sea!

1.2.3 Counting under the sea!

© 2016 by Peggy Sue Brown. All rights reserved.
Illustrations by Kyle Csortos

This book is dedicated to my grandsons Carson and Joshua.
~I will always be your stars beside the moon~ Peggy Sue Brown
Special Thank You Nancy Gene Nickerson, friends and family
for encouraging me to follow my dream.

ISBN: 1533200939

1

WHALE

2

SHARKS

3

MANATEES

4

OCTOPI

5

HORSESHOE CRABS

6

EELS

7

CRABS

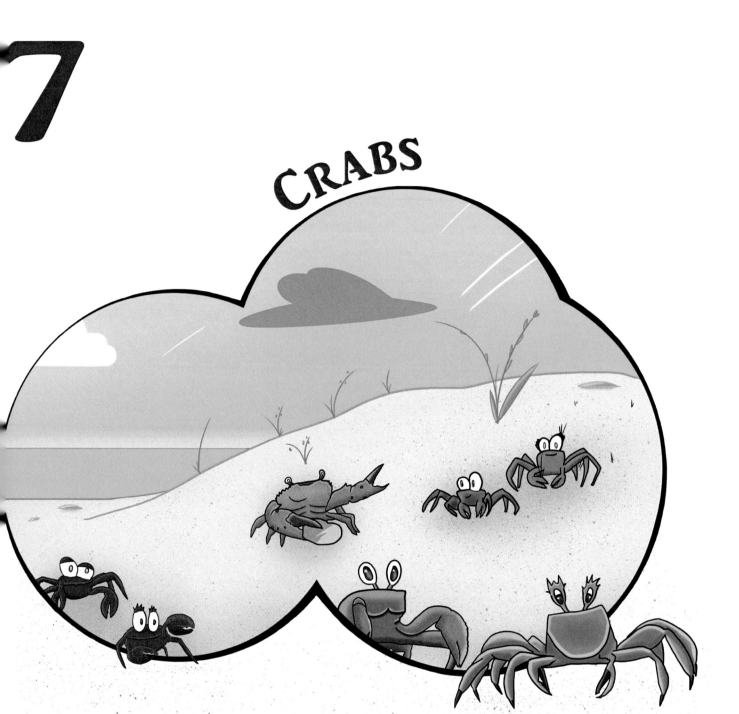

8

SEA TURTLES

9

GUITAR FISH

10

STINGRAYS

11

DOLPHINS

BUTTERFLY FISH

PUFFER FISH

14

SAND DOLLARS

PARROT FISH

16

17

ANGELFISH

18

SEA SNAILS

19

JELLYFISH

20

SEAHORSES

FUN FACTS!

1. Right Whales can survive up to be 70 years old. They reach up to 50 feet and weigh up to 70 tons. Right whales eat zooplankton and krill. They were named Right whales because they were the "right" whale t hunt and were so easy to catch and pull to shore. Right whales are the most endangered of all whales an only several hundred are left in the world.

2. (A) Blacknose Sharks live up to be 20 years old. They can range from 4-4 ½ feet long and weigh around 2 pounds. Blacknose sharks eat fish and cephalopods. They have 11-13 rows of teeth on their upper and lowe jaws and are near threatened.
    (B) Atlantic Sharpnose Sharks live to be 12 years old, can reach up to 2 ½ feet long, and weigh up to 16 pound Atlantic Sharpnose sharks eat small fish and crustaceans. Their snout is parabolic and they are considered to b a species of "least concern".

3. Manatees live to be 60 years old, can be as long as 12 feet, and weigh more than 1000 pounds. They ar strict herbivores. Manatees were mistaken for mermaids and are listed as endangered animals.

4. Octopi only live from a couple months to a few years. They grow to fit their environment and are large in cold water compared to being smaller in tropical or warm waters. They have 3 hearts, blue blood, and ar not endangered or threatened.

5. Horseshoe Crabs can live up to be 40 years old, reach up to 24 inches, and weigh about 2-10 pound. The eat worms, algae, clams, and mussels. Horseshoe crabs are called the living fossil, have 9 eyes, and are nea threatened.

6. Eels have a life span of about 85 years old. They can reach over 12 feet long and weigh on an average 3 pounds. Eels eat lobster, fish, octopi, crabs, mussels, snails, and frog. Eels can swim forwards and backwards Some species are listed as endangered.

7. Crabs live to be 4 years old. They range from ¼ inch to 12 feet long and weigh up to 10 pounds. Crab eat algae, fungi, bacteria, crustaceans, mollusks, and worms. Crabs appeared on earth 200 million years ag and some species are listed as endangered.

8. Sea Turtles can live up to be 80 years old. They can be 30 inches to 16 feet long and weigh up to 100 pounds. Sea turtles eat sea grass, crabs, clams, jellyfish, and sea cucumbers. Sea turtles have lived on eartl for more than 220 million years and 6 out of the 7 species are listed as endangered.

9. Shovelnose Guitarfish live to be about 16 years old. They can reach up to 11 feet long, weigh up to 3 pounds, and eat fish, decapods, and shrimp. Shovelnose Guitarfish are totally harmless to humans and are near threatened.

10. Stingrays can live up to be 25 years old. They can reach up to 6 ½ feet in length, weigh up to 79 pounds, and eat clams, shrimp, and mussels. Stingray mouths are located at the bottom of their body and some of the 60 different species are threatened.

FUN FACTS!

1. Dolphins live up to be 50 years old. They can reach up to 30 feet long, range from 90 pounds to 11 tons, and eat fish, squid, seals, sea lions, other dolphins, and whales. The Killer Whale or Orca is a species of dolphin and several dolphin species could be extinct in the near future.

2. Butterfly Fish live up to be 7 years old in the wild and up to 10 years old in captivity. They can reach up to 8 inches long and weigh less than a pound. Butterfly fish eat algae, seaweed, worms, small crustaceans, and zooplankton. They are diurnal and are on the endangered species list.

3. Puffer Fish can live up to 10 years of age and there are 120 different species. They range in size from 1 inch to 2 feet long and can weigh up to 30 pounds. Puffer fish eat mussels, clams, shellfish, algae, worms, and crustaceans. Sharks are the only species immune to the Puffer fish toxin and even though they are stable in the wild Puffer fish are considered to be vulnerable.

4. Sand Dollars can survive up to 6-10 years old. They are usually 3 inches wide and eat plankton, crustacean larvae, copepods, algae, and diatoms. Sand dollars can chew food for up to 15 minutes before swallowing. The number of growth rings on the Sand dollar plates indicates their age. Sand dollars are numerous and widespread in the ocean.

5. Parrot Fish can live to be 5-15 years. They range from less than 1 foot to 4 feet long, weigh up to 45 pounds, and eat algae extracted from chunks of coral ripped from a reef. They wear "pajamas" at night and some species are vulnerable or endangered.

6. Sea Stars (also known as star fish however are not related to fish at all) can live up to 35 years in age. They can be 5-10 inches long and weigh up to 11 pounds. Sea stars eat clams, shells, and mussels. Sea stars can grow their arms back if one is lost and they are not endangered.

7. Angelfish can live up to be 15 years old. They can reach 2 to 24 inches in length and weigh up to 2 pounds. Marine Angelfish eat sponges, algae, jellyfish, and small fish while the freshwater Angelfish eat bloodworm, shrimp, and insects. Newly hatched Angelfish are called a Fry and they are not endangered.

8. Sea Snails are so great in variability that generalization about life span, size, and feeding are not possible. Their shells have been used for jewelry from prehistoric times to modern days. The Ribbed Mediterranean Limpet is one of the most endangered Sea snails and is listed as being in danger of extinction.

9. Jellyfish live from several hours to several months depending on the species. They can range from the size of a pinhead to almost 8 feet wide. Jellyfish eat phytoplankton, copepods, fish eggs, larvae of different species, and other jellyfish. They appeared on Earth before the dinosaurs and there are 350 different species. Jellyfish are not listed as endangered.

20. Seahorses can live 1-5 years. They can range from ½ inch to 14 inches and weigh 1 gram to 2 pounds. Seahorses eat plankton and small crustaceans. They are the slowest swimmers in the ocean and can swim as slow as 5 feet per hour. Some species of the seahorse is endangered.

AUTHOR
PEGGY SUE BROWN

THE INSPIRATION FOR THIS BOOK:

THE MARINE SCIENCE CENTER

HTTP://WWW.MARINESCIENCECENTER.COM/

JIM SAWGRASS NATIVE AMERICAN HISTORIAN

HTTP://WWW.JIMSAWGRASS.COM/

SAVE THE MANATEE CLUB

HTTP://WWW.SAVETHEMANATEE.ORG/

HTTP://ORIGINAL.LIVESTREAM.COM/SAVETHEMANATEECAM

HTTPS://WWW.FLORIDASTATEPARKS.ORG/PARK/BLUE-SPRING

Wylie,

My wish for you is to
find a miracle everyday
in life and in reading

Peggy Sue
Dean

Made in the USA
Middletown, DE
27 June 2016